For my three remarkable children, Saul, Ashey, and JoJo,
who showed me how to build into the waves
JABL

To Lian and Ted and our summer in Cape Cod
QL

Candlewick Press, 99 Dover Street, Somerville, Massachusetts 02144. www.candlewick.com.
Printed in Humen, Dongguan, China. 22 23 24 25 26 27 APS 10 9 8 7 6 5 4 3 2 1

A DAY FOR SANDCASTLES

JonArno Lawson

illustrated by Qin Leng

CANDLEWICK PRESS

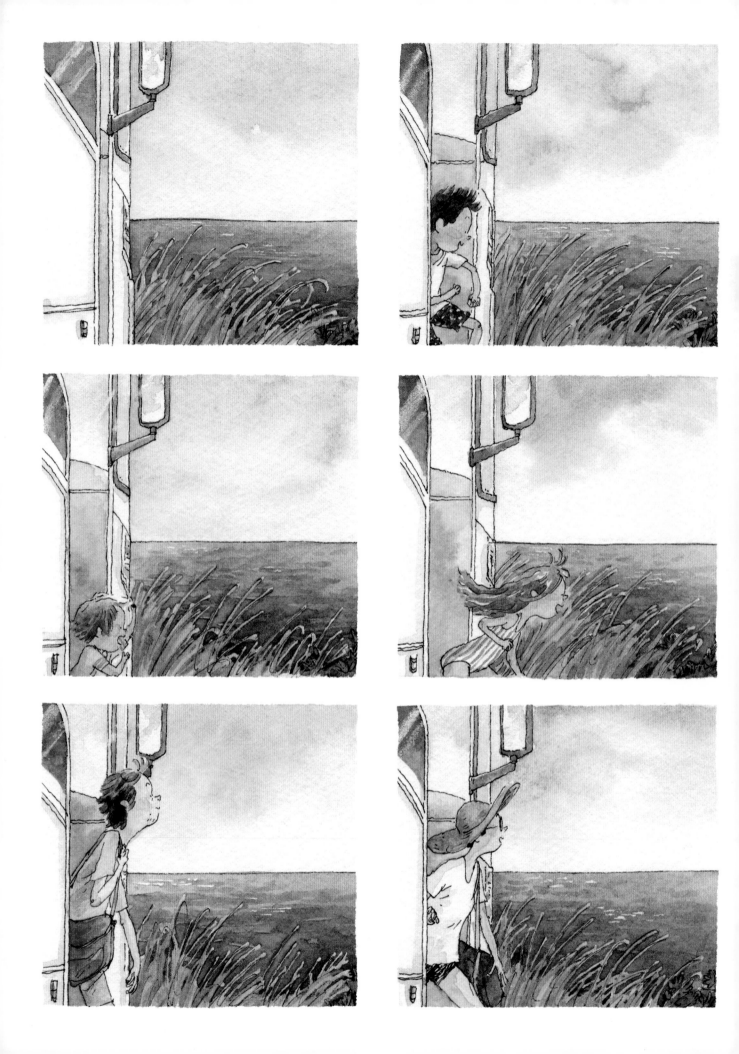